Winter in Harmattan
and
Other Short Stories

Prince E.A.J. Kenny

Sierra Leonean Writers Series

Warima/Freetown/Accra
120 Kissy Road, Freetown, Sierra Leone
Kofi Annan Ave, North Legon, Accra, Ghana
Publisher: Prof. Osman Sankoh (Mallam O.)
publisher@sl-writers-series.org
www.sl-writers-series.org

Winter in Harmattan and Other Short Stories

Copyright © 2017 by Prince E.A.J. Kenny
All rights reserved.

ISBN: 978-9988-8698-2-3

Sierra Leonean Writers Series

Dedication

This collection of short stories is dedicated to all who witnessed and survived the Ebola epidemic in Sierra Leone and all lovers of literature.

Contents

Endorsements..iii

Foreword v

Summary.. vi

Winter in

Harmattan.. 1

The Lockdown 14

Emancipated 26

The Final Call..39

Moving On...59

Endorsements

Mr. Kenny has demonstrated mastery in presenting very interesting and memorable events in his short stories collection. His detailed description of events in the short stories makes reading easier and gives the reader the desire to read on and learn more. The collection can also be recommended for study in schools and other institutions of learning not only in Sierra Leone but also in other countries across the world.

Dr. Moira Ferran
Lecturer in French,
Fourah Bay College – University of Sierra Leone

Prince Kenny's *Winter in Harmattan and other stories* can be considered as one of contemporary time. This can be justified by the well-described and sequenced narration of events which also brings out themes such as patience, love, perseverance and piousness. In the current *Global Village* we live, such values are required for growth and development and that is what Prince has skilfully conveyed to his readers in his collection.

Issa Roberts
Lecturer in Linguistics
Fourah Bay College – University of Sierra Leone

From his childhood, Prince had a knack for telling stories which were appreciated by his colleagues and relatives. Growing up, the passion metamorphosed and it is a great honour to read Prince Kenny's Collection of stories which is very interesting and educative. I am confident that Prince will not only stop at this publication but do more in order to make Sierra Leonean literature popular.

Emma, Gloria Dupigny (Mrs.)
Ex-Principal- Methodist Boys' High School
Kissy Mess-Mess
Freetown, Sierra Leone

Prince Kenny has indeed manifested his passion for creative writing which he has nurtured over the years. His resilience in life has made him rise to this level and I have no doubt that he will do more to propagate Sierra Leonean Literature. I am proud of my ex-pupil and wish him continued success.

Hectora Pyne-Bailey (Mrs)
Ex- teacher, Prince of Wales Secondary School
Current Senior Admnisitrative Officer, Institute of Public Administration and Management – USL

Acknowledgements

I am indebted to the following individuals whose expertise in proofreading my several drafts of my work has resulted in the publication:

Dr. Stephen Ney
Dr. Momodu Turay
Dr. Moira Ferran
Mr. Desmond George-Williams
Mr. Ambrose T. Rogers
Mr. Issa Roberts

I am conscious of the fact that they have spent hours going through the different stories in order to get the end product. I am grateful and pray for God's continued widom and strength in all their daily endeavours.

Foreword

In the next few years, you will no doubt find yourself faced with dozens of books about the Ebola epidemic in Sierra Leone from 2014-15. They will give you more than enough information about its causes and consequences, its medical, political and cultural aspects, as well as lessons learned and those still to be learned.

But what did it feel like to be in Sierra Leone during that difficult time? It must have been both fearful and sad; but what were the manifestations of the fear and the sadness in the thoughts and actions of ordinary Sierra Leoneans? How did the "winter" of Ebola affect human relationships, and – we must ask this question even as we acknowledge irreparable losses – what valuable insight did it generate? What did Ebola reveal about the human condition that might otherwise have remained hidden?

If these questions interest you as they interest me, then *Winter in Harmattan and other stories* might be the most interesting book you will find on Ebola and other issues about life. And of course it is about much more than just Ebola: it is about education and its costs, marriage and its stresses, coping with difficult situations, God and His unendingly surprising power to answer prayer as it is about families and friendships.

Mr Kenny has put his considerable skills of social observation and verbal expression to good use in these five short stories, which I hope will find a wide readership both in Sierra Leone and abroad.

Dr. Stephen Ney
Lecturer, Language Studies Department, FBC/

Introduction

"Winter in Harmattan" and other stories present contemporary issues which bring out many lessons concerning marriage, health and safety, bereavement and successes as well as other challenges in life.

In "Winter in Harmattan" the protagonist Samrold had planned to spend Christmas with his parents in Africa and at the same time celebrate his success in academia; having obtained his PhD from one of the renowned universities in America. That was disrupted by a deadly disease affecting the citizens in the country (Losa), where his parents lived. Consequently, all preparations were stalled due to a State of Emergency declared by Losa President two days before the event.

The LOCK DOWN gives an account of one of the measures taken by the government of a particular country to combat the Ebola which was devastating that country. As the plot unfolds, citizens had to prepare for the LOCKDOWN as it was to last for three days. Mr and Mrs Jimrince Ota were among those who tried to stock the necessary commodity that would sustain them throughout the period when all and sundry prayed for its end.

In the story titled *"Emancipated"*, the protagonist Pearlmira Kentuckey had a divine answer to prayers when she met Jim Wotah. The former had thought that she would never get married as she had passed the expected age for young women to get married. Jim's presence in her life and later proposal to marry her came as a great relief to the Kentuckey family.

The marriage was celebrated in grand style as both parties had wanted and at the same time, both families displayed their wealth.

In the story titled *"The Final Call"* the author vividly brings out the pains and sadness in losing a dear one. Daisyclair, the protagonist was devastated when the news of her husband's death was announced as she had been in marriage with Ekundayo for 26 years before death struck. The story also brings out the importance of the community when such events take place and how they helped in alleviating the sorrow of parting which Daisyclair and her family were going through. On the other side of the coin, one can see the unity and cooperation from family members – especially Daisyclair's brothers and other relatives – who supported their sister during her bereavement. The author also elucidates tension during such events as represented by Ekundayo's cousins who had some other motive when they visited Daisyclair on hearing about the demise of their cousin Ekundayo.

Moving on, the final story in this collection, focuses on the reward for hard work. Cornelius, the protagonist, experienced God's divine favour in everything he did and due to his outstanding performance in the discharge of his duty, he was respected by everyone he came across.

Winter in Harmattan

When November announced itself that year, everyone in Losa country had very high hopes that cases of infected persons of the dreaded disease would drop significantly. This was the wish of all and sundry in Losa because they wanted to spend Christmas in the usual pomp and pageantry. To show how enthusiastic Losanians were, some had started preparations for the traditional carnivals. Others who loved swimming and adventure were planning beach outings and other related sprees in order to celebrate the Yuletide like they used to. Others still were thinking of travelling to the province or to neighbouring countries to celebrate the Christmas vacation.

One such family preparing for the celebration was the Melasis. They had high hopes of celebrating Christmas that year because their only child had graduated from the University of California in October that year and they were longing to have him celebrate the success in Losa.

Samrold had earlier promised his parents that he would come to celebrate the event with them as he had been away from home for a very long time as he had relocated to the United States of America fifteen years earlier. More than a decade earlier, Samrold had wanted to visit his parents to celebrate Christmas but was unable to do so owing to a bloody civil war, still ravaging, at the time of his intended visit. His absence that year had had a negative impact on his parents who had made plans to welcome their son, who had just gained admission to university. The events that year turned sour for the Melasis and that great disappointment was likened to a

2

situation in which winter had come during the Harmattan.

This time round, Mr and Mrs. Melasis were not willing to have a repeat of the incident and hoped that things would be different. In fact, they were more optimistic about a rapid end of the dreaded disease than most of their neighbours. To show how enthusiastic they were about this move, they had intensified night prayer meetings to seek God's intervention against the deadly disease which was ravaging their country. Mr Melasis, being a statistician, was also attentive to the daily update of infected persons on radio and television, following which, would do an analysis of the situation to know whether the disease was stabilizing or not. .

One night, while sitting with his wife Anthea, he expressed a lot of optimism about the infection rate in the country and even made a forecast that the disease would have been completely eradicated before the start of the new month. That pronouncement sparked off a challenging debate between the two and they ended on a high note that no matter what, their son would come and celebrate his PhD with them. Having a PhD in Education was no mean achievement for the Melasis as they had always believed that the best way to success was through hard work. Thus, they never encouraged their son to be idle or to seek material gains. While he was still in Losa, Mrs. Anthea Melasis would from time to time buy educative books for her son and they ranged from the most academic to the most relaxing. For her, their only son was the joy and pride and they wanted him to become an icon in society. Even Mr. Melasis would buy interesting videos of some of the novels he studied while in Losa or borrow some from the nearby library. All was done to make Samrold comfortable with his studies.

Indeed, that dream had been achieved and here was Samrold, a proud holder of a Doctorate in Education. As she pondered over her son's resounding success and imminent celebration, she recalled once when Samrold was to represent his school at an Inter-School debate. Being an outstanding pupil, the school authority together with his parents was confident that he was going to win the competition. Fate, however, struck that morning as Samrold could not give the right answers to two of the quiz questions. He had come second and his close friend Justin, who was attending another prestigious private school, had narrowly beaten him.

That incident deflated Samrold's moral and confidence for a whole week. He did not attend school for that week in fearing he would be booed at by his classmates and close friends. When he overcame his trauma, Samrold vowed that no one would ever beat him in any competition. It was as if God answered his prayers, for he was always first in all the competitions at which he represented his school until he graduated from High School. Whenever he won, he would come home very happy and, before sharing the good news with his parents, he would first of all go to his bedroom to thank and praise God for granting him divine favour. Knowing this routine, the parents never disturbed him whenever he returned from any competition.

As the days went by, the Melasis continued making the preparations. In California, Samrold had also been putting things in place for the meeting with his parents. In fact, he had already shipped a container of goods they would need for the big party to be thrown in his honour.

By the end of November that year, the situation had still not improved. The cases of newly-infected persons had risen by thirty percent and that was no good news for anyone especially the Melasis. One evening, while the Melasis were watching television, there was a press release from the State House that a State of Emergency had been proclaimed and consequently, no public gatherings or other related programmes were to take place for the three months following the Press Release. Moreover, there was an addendum stating that market days were reduced to six instead of seven. Sunday trading was completely banned and even trading on Saturdays was restricted. Traders had to stop selling before midday as no one was permitted to sell after midday.

The proclamation that night brought about a graveyard silence in their house and there was no need for further debate on the liberty to celebrate Christmas that year. They immediately decided to retire to bed because the news had dampened their enthusiasm.

The following morning, Mrs. Melasis woke up feeling terribly ill.. Fortunately for her, her husband rushed to the nearby pharmacy to buy the required medication. She was advised by her husband to rest while the maid did all the necessary domestic duties.

The President's press release was also a subject of concern in the neighbourhood. One such concerned individual was Muctarr, President of the Democrats Social Club. This club had been in existence for more than a decade and their contribution towards education in Losa had been immense. In fact, for the past eight years, they had been awarding scholarships to less fortunate pupils in both primary and secondary schools. Most of the proceeds the received from programmes organized was used to sponsor their educational programmes. They were also planning the traditional outing to the famous Kalaka beach on Boxing Day that year. He was so worried that he could not eat the whole day. As night was falling, he decided to call his Vice-President – Bakisa – to share his concerns. When Bakisa saw Muctarr's number on her phone, she thought he was still ill as three days earlier, he had been complaining of a serious stomach ache. When she finally received the call, her first statement was:

"Muctarr, are you still ill? Why don't you go and see a doctor?"

"Bakisa that is not the problem. I'm much better now. Like you advised the last time we spoke, I saw the doctor who prescribed some treatment for me. In addition, he advised me to be drinking a lot of fluids and I have decided that I would take at least five litres of water a day.

"So how are you feeling now after taking the treatment"

"Sister, I told you I'm ok now."

"I thank God for you now!"

"Yea. Thanks for the concern. However, I have been preoccupied since last night when the State of Emergency was announced."

"Say it again Muctarr! I myself have been worried since I heard the announcement. What are we going to do? You know that we have sold a lot of tickets for the outing!"

"Well, let's pray for a miracle before mid December. You know we have paid for the buses to take our guests to the beach and the bus company may not be willing to refund the money we have paid."

"You're right, but we should start thinking about a plan B to avoid any embarrassment."

"So true Bakisa. Why not think about organizing an Inter-Area quiz competition and debate and get school-going children and students in tertiary institutions involved? After all, our organization does promote education in spite of the fact that it is socially inclined and you know the number of pupils from various regions in the country have benefited from our benevolence.

"I've no problems with that. Muctarr, don't you understand public gatherings are forbidden? Doing such would be gross disrespect for law and order in the country and we may likely face the penalty"

"There you go again, my sister. I'm really confused now. The only option now is prayer for divine intervention. We should declare a period of fasting and cry to the God of heaven to take away this plague from our land. Maybe that will help us to think straight."

"Thanks so much for the call and have a pleasant evening!"

7

"Don't mention it my sister. Should you think of any other plan, don't hesitate to call me. I am always at your beck and call."

When he finished talking on the phone, Muctarr heard a strange knock on his door. He kept wondering who it was especially when it was late in the night. Even though he was still sleepy, he opened the door. To his greatest surprise, he saw Aunty Maria, who lived five doors away from him. She had been one of the pillars in the community as she was always involved in promoting women's and girls' issues. She was working for a renowned Non-Governmental Organization which advocated for women's and girls' rights. She was very pleased to come to Muctarr and without wasting time, shetold him why she had come so late.

"Good evening Muctarr.

"Good evening aunty Maria.

"Sorry for coming at this time of the night because such night visits are unusual these days."

"Don't mention it, Ma. Is there anything I can do for you, Ma?

"Well, really son. I came just to seek some advice on the press release and s grand exhibition that my friends and I are planning. You know that I have been in the fashion business for over two decades and every year, we organize such exhibitions to raise funds to help those suffering from breast cancer which is of great concern to many women."

"Thanks so much for considering me as one who could influence your decisions but honestly, Ma, if you had come about five minutes earlier, you would have met me on the telephone with the Vice-President of my social organization. We are faced with a similar problem as we have an outing planned for Boxing Day and as of today, the situation does not seem to be improving. Rather, it's getting worse." We too are very worried as we have sold out a number of tickets to our guests.

"Son, the problem is that we have ordered and paid for a lot of clothing from different African designers for the week-long event. With this dreadful disease, I am not sure that the programme will take place.

"That's the problem we all face now, Ma, as we've made huge financial investments with the aim of recovering at least the capital from our different planned programmes. One thing I would suggest is that we form a network of prayer warriors and pray for God's timely as he is the only one we can depend on now.

"I think that's a good idea. Can you coordinate that for me?"

"No problem, Ma. I'll contact other interested neighbours and we can start soonest.

"Thanks, son, and have a goodnight's rest!"

When she left him, Muctarr locked the door to his room and fell asleep instantly. He had been so tired that day that he slept like a newborn baby. His immediate neighbours could hear him snore like an old steam engine trying to climb a hill.

For the next two weeks, everyone went about their daily activities with some amount of hope that a miracle would happen and that the disease would be completely eradicated before Christmas. Muctarr and some neighbours had continued their daily prayers as was suggested by aunty Maria. The health workers also did their best to see to it that the number of cases dropped. By the end of November, the cases had really declined. When the first week of December ended, the daily updates were still favourable and some kind of renewed hope had been born in the hearts and minds of Losanians. Being confident about the lifting of the State of Health Emergency before Christmas, Muctarr and his executive recommenced their plans for the Boxing Day outing. They went to print out more tickets as the ones they had earlier printed had sold out.

The Melasis were also hopeful and continued their plans. In fact, Mrs. Melasis seized the opportunity to distribute the invitations they had printed much earlier, to the people they wanted to invite to the all-important graduation party. As if the distribution of the invitations did not satisfy them, Mr. Melasis ordered some souvenir items for the occasion. He had to pay extra for the items because he told the person in charge that he would like to have unique items. Thus, the wall clocks with their son's picture engraved, as well as the CD recording of some of their son's favourite songs, would definitely come as a surprise to Samrold, who would never have expected his parents to go the extra mile to please him.

When Samrold called home that week and the good news about the declining number of new cases was announced, he finally became resolute that he should buy his return ticket no matter the cost.

By the start of the third week of December, the story changed as the number of new infected persons became very alarming to the government officials. This was because some people who had clandestine party a few days earlier. The interaction was so great that some people who had the disease at incubating stage inadvertently infected others. The government officials were rather worried; the President summoned an emergency Cabinet meeting where a national Lockdown over the Christmas period was decided. Even though the measure was tough, yet it had to be done to save the country from more deaths the disease brought.

Two days to Christmas, Losanians were informed that the President would make a public announcement on Christmas Eve at around 9:00 am. Everyone was anxious to listen to him. Some Losanians were surprised about the time change because the President normally gave his Message on Christmas Day.

At 9:00 am, everyone was glued to his radio ready to listen to the President. The tail end of the speech shocked everyone as the President said:

"We as a government tried our best to put an end to this deadly disease before the Christmas celebrations, but as a result of some irresponsible individuals, the number of new cases has resurged. In view of this, a complete Lockdown will be observed from 25th December to 2nd January. Let me wish you all a Merry Christmas in advance and a bright and prosperous New year."

Mr. and Mrs. Melasis could not believe their ears. Was the President joking? Or was he trying to be diplomatic? Samrold was to arrive on the evening of the 24th and everything was set. What could they do when everything had been paid for? In fact Mr. Melasis had collected the souvenir items as well as the shipped items from the

United States of America the day before the President's message. For the second time since Samrold's departure, both of them were stunned.

Mrs. Melasis fainted, but luckily, her husband and the maid rushed her to the nearby clinic. Although being Christmas Eve, most of the doctors were not on duty. Fortunately, Mr. Melasis remembered that his nephew was also a qualified cardiologist, so he decided to call him. When he arrived, he ordered the nurse to increase the dose of her medication. By 4:00 pm, Mrs. Melasis had recovered and not wanting to spend Christmas in the clinic, pleaded with her husband to take her home. The husband heeded her plea as he would not like Samrold to find his darling mother in the hospital.

Indeed, Samrold arrived that night as flights were still operating in spite of the President's proclamation. The welcome was not as rousing as they had planned. When he heard about his mother's illness, Samrold burst into tears. He cried so loudly that the neighbours heard him. One of them came over and tried to console him. Given the state he was in, Samrold had to take some sedative.

Christmas day was quietly spent at home. As he had lost his appetite, Samrold asked the maid to prepare him something which would help him regain his appetite. After eating, he went back to sleep.

When he woke up later in the evening, he realized his mother was much better. For the first time in fifteen years, Samrold hugged his mother and a very long conversation followed. The father was happy to participate in the conversation even though all they had prepared was wasted.

During the days which followed, Samrold did not do anything much. He slept a lot and when he woke up, would find something to eat and then watched movies. One night however, he decided to attend choir practice in his church. He saw his old friends Mike and Jonathan and after practice, the latter accompanied Samrold home. They chatted throughout the night on issues ranging from those of interest to absurd issues. At dawn, Mrs. Melasis ordered the maid to prepare a very sumptuous breakfast for Samrold's friends who had become great men in their society.

They promised the Melasis that they would continue to keep in touch even after their friend Samrold returned to the United States of America.

Upon leaving, Samrold gave them the gifts he had bought for them and they were very much appreciative of the kind gesture of someone they considered a brother.

The Lockdown

The atmosphere was calm that Saturday evening as Mr. and Mrs. Jimrince Ota watched television in silence. It was raining heavily like the previous night. At 9:00 p.m. the evening news came on and just after the news, there was a Press Release. The release stated that there would be a three-day nationwide Lockdown the following week to control the deadly disease which was ravaging the country. The Ebola disease which started in May that year, was still claiming the lives of many citizens. Initially, many people took the issue lightly. Among those who trivialized the outbreak were diehard traditionalists and illiterates who said that many people were dying in rural areas because of an evil spell. Another school of thought was that a "Witch Plane" had crashed and those who were dying were passengers onboard the plane. The belief is that witches and wizards make use of different objects for their nocturnal activities. Among those are paw-paw and ground nut shells. Thus, if anything contrary happens, the object will crash and that would be responsible for a high number of deaths. Therefore, those who trivialized the outbreak were referring to the plane crash.

A "Witch Plane" according them, is any *local* device used by sorcerers to go on their nocturnal activities and may range from groundnut shells to pawpaw or any other thing the sorcerer may decide to use.

Later, when the disease was getting out of hand, the government decided to take a robust approach. This nationwide Lockdown was supposed to be a tough reaction to the epidemic.

Mr. Ota was shocked when he heard the release because he knew that poverty was widespread and people had to fend hard to earn a living He wondered how people in the country would cope with a three-day shut down. As for Mrs. Ellen Ota, sounded very doubtful because the last time the government proclaimed a one-day "Sit-in and Reflection" at national level, it was very stressful to many citizens who had not been in a position to stock food. She remembered how she had to shared food and potable water so that neighbours who were less privileged.

As the days of the countdown to the lockdown went by, there were conflicting comments and views from near and far on issues ranging from security, to food and other survival measures. Radio and television broadcasts during that period were all geared towards addressing the concerns raised by the citizens. As for traders and other business-minded people, they were convinced that it was the opportune moment for them to make considerable profit like they had done during the preparation and observance of Ramadan three months earlier.

Mrs. Ota therefore seized the opportunity to go shopping three days before the lockdown. As she walked along the famous Vodacot market where prices were relatively low, she met her best friend Canishia, the current Minister of Housing in their country. She was shocked to see her at that market because Canishia was considered part of society's crème de la crème and as such did all her shopping at the Prixon supermarket where most of the government officials and expatriates shopped. In order to satisfy her curiosity, she engaged her friend in a conversation

"Canishia, I'm surprised to see you here Market at this time, and moreover, without a police escort. What's wrong?"

"Ellen my sister, nothing is wrong. I am fine just like you. The reason for my visit to Vodacot market is that most of the prices at Prixon supermarket, where I normally shop, have sky-rocketed and you know I have to cut my coat according to my size. You should also be aware of the fact that the current epidemic has greatly affected the economic situation countrywide and we have to cope with it.

"You can say that again my sister. Even in this market, prices too have escalated. I wonder why the increase? We are really not very patriotic, because traders are bent on exploiting buyers regardless of the present situation. Where are we going with such an attitude?"

"Nowhere, sister. If we start discussing this issue, we won't buy anything. I would rather advise that we leave the issue at this point and then continue our different shopping exercises."

"Indeed, this is a wise idea. Let me wish you a pleasant day and may God keep us safe from this deadly epidemic!"

At this, they went their separate ways. Ellen had to go to different stalls to get all that they would need in the house during the Lockdown because she would not like any food shortage during the period. As she walked out of the market towards her vehicle, parked in the next corner, she met another friend – Mrs. Jeredine Manneh.

who had come to shop for her husband and three children. She was dressed like an astronaut going into space. Ellen Ota was surprised to see her friend dressed in that gear and curiosity made her engage her in a conversation.

"My sister, when did you come from the tenth planet? Don't you think that you have arrived on planet Earth?"

"Ellen, I have never gone to the tenth planet. I've always been on this planet but the reason for my peculiar gear is to protect myself against the deadly disease which is causing so much harm. The area where I live is among the most vulnerable and I have to be extremely cautious. Imagine, just yesterday, someone died from the disease in my neighbourhood and you could imagine the shock and panic which swept the area. The only option for us was to pray, as prayer is now considered the last resort. I have now come to buy some provisions to sustain us for the next three days which our government has declared as a period of Lockdown."

"Then rush and get what you want before everything runs out in the market! As it stands, the traders have wilfully raised prices. How can the poor survive now that prices have considerably changed?"

"That is the same question I'm asking but the good Book tells us that God is our hope and strength and a very present help in trouble. Our hope is now solidly built on God for He is our trust in time of need.

"So true, sister. Anyway, we will continue to keep in touch on the phone. Bye."

By the time Ellen got to the car, it was almost half past six and as usual, the traffic congestion had begun. The snail-paced drive from one point to the other made her feel disgusted and vowed not to come out of her house for the next two weeks. Her feet were full of muck as she had to manage to get through the crowd at Vodacot market while she shopped.

There was also a crowd of people who scrambled to board the few public transports available. This scarcity in public transportation came about two weeks earlier when the government and other stakeholders, as part of measures put in place to curb the epidemic, decided to cut down on the number of passengers allowed in the different public vehicles.

The days following were days full of anxiety and gloom. Some people thought that the Lockdown would be an avenue for crime; for according to rumours, medical personnel who would visit homes would inject anyone looking ill with a kind of poison and the inmate would later die. Others still had to go the extra mile in search of funds to stock essential foodstuffs before the start of the process.

In fact, most offices had changed their hours of operation. For instance, the banking sector had changed operation hours from 09:30 to 15:00 to 08:30 to 13:30 with a view to allowing its workers to finish early and get to their residence before dusk which was normally scary. The use of chlorine, hand sanitizers and other potent disinfectants in all public places and most dwelling houses had been spontaneously adopted about eight weeks earlier. However, bulk purchase of these items was evident a day to the Lockdown.

On the eve of the Lockdown, most offices closed even earlier than usual. It was as if the Prophetic Rapture was going to take place the following day and everyone was trying to be prepared. The bakeries were overcrowded Other food items had also become so scarce; the irony was that even though people had money to purchase such items, they were unable to do so. Transportation was another problem because the few in operation could not meet the high demand to convey commuters to their various destinations. Some vehicle drivers seized the opportunity to exploit commuters by raising the fares considerably. That did not stop determined commuters to board the minibuses and taxis available. Others who could not afford the new fares were obliged to walk to their destinations to get home before the 20:00 hours deadline which had earlier been communicated on the media.

By 19:30, everyone had returned home and the streets were deserted as they had been during the rebel war in that country some 20 years back. Even the dogs and cats were sensitive to the stillness and one could clearly hear a pin should anyone inadvertently dropped it. The appointed 20:00 hours finally came and the President gave a very challenging message which urged citizens to respect the directives given for the Lockdown so that the dreadful disease would finally be controlled.

The following day was day one of the Lockdown and at the Ota's, all was quiet as they fasted and prayed till lunch time. Mr. Ota was the one who presided over that morning's devotion. He started with a wonderful and spirit-filled praise and worship session before moving on to the prayer session. When he started praying, one could hear his faltering voice while he implored God to save his family, protect citizens and destroy the deadly disease. The thunderous amen by his wife came as a backup to the prayer and if it were possible to see heaven, one may have seen the pleasing countenance of the Most Gracious God as He inhabited the praises and supplication of His children. Similar situations were observed in the neighbourhood because the Otas could hear singing in the neighbourhood.

As there was no breakfast for them that morning, due to the fasting they had decided on, they tuned in to various radio stations in for pertinent information on the Lockdown and sensitization exercise. The news was not good that day; while most people stayed home, some walked the streets and sat at street junctions to while away time. The news was not well received by the media as they considered those defaulters to be anti-government.

It was also disheartening to hear that the sensitization team members were facing a lot of constraints. Some teams did not have enough soap to give to the different households they visited. Others did not even start the exercise on time while others still were deliberately sidelined after their training because they had no connections among those recruiting. They had to be replaced by relatives and close friends of their supervisors and coordinators.

However, on a more positive note, some areas were visited by the sensitization team who gave them the desired information on the epidemic. In addition, bars of soap were given to each household visited and though minimal, some appreciated the gesture while those with larger families would have wanted more than one bar of soap.

In the evening, when the Otas tuned in to the news, they were given an update on the first day's exercise and though it was not completely favourable, they were pleased at the fact that some progress had been made.

Day two of the LockDown was better than the previous day. The sun was shining brighter than it did on the day before and there was no power cut which was not the case the day earlier. As usual, the Otas continued their fasting and praying. At around 09:30 am, the sensitization team arrived at their residence. Being very wary of the process, they decided not to allow the team in the house for fear of being contaminated by anyone. Mr. Ota, a renowned medical practitioner, was very tactful in asking questions about the mode of transmission of the virus as well as ways of prevention. When the ten-minute dialogue ended, the Otas were given a bar of soap as prescribed by officials of the Emergency Operation Centre. In fact, one of the members of the sensitization team became interested in Mr. Ota's questions and interrogated if the latter was a medical personnel. Mr. Ota's response was in the affirmative and Joseph, the individual, told him that he would like to have Mr. Ota as his friend.

Two hours later, Mrs. Ellen Ota's phone rang. It was her mother-in-law who was calling to check on them. Ellen had been a very nice daughter-in-law to the Otas and they were all glad when their son and brother Jimrince married Ellen five years earlier.

"Mama we are doing fine. Your son is more than ok." was Ellen's reply.

"My daughter, I have no doubts in you. If the family had not trusted you, we would not have given our consent to Jimrince marrying you."

"I know Mama. That is why you will be my mother till death. In some family circles, the wife is never at peace with her in-laws but it is the contrary in my own case because your son and you all have proved your undying love for me."

"Ok, my daughter. Thank you"

"Not at all, Mama. The pleasure is mine. Let me pass you on to Jimrince."

Indeed, the phone was passed on to Jimrince and after another three minutes of chat with his mother, he hung up.

At midday, they broke the fast for that day. While they were having lunch, they seized the opportunity to watch the national television for a news update. It was then they realized that some suspected victims had been taken to treatment centres. Others who had died on the streets were tested to find out whether they had died of the disease. The rather sad sight was pathetic but courage, from both the personnel on duty and relatives of the victims, was needed. The rest of the day was spent in silence and meditation as there was not much to do. As a way of overcoming their boredom and as a way of keeping their spirits alive, the couple decided to watch some movies at dusk.

The third day was sunnier than the two previous days. In addition, it was a Sunday and as a means of giving the Christians the opportunity to worship their God, the early radio broadcasts that morning were all Christian related; preaching, prayer sessions and other spirit–filled programmes were broadcast live, involving various religious in the country. It was no coincidence that all the messages spoke of courage and perseverance to become victorious in spite of the pestilence in the country. This spiritual exercise coincided with the Otas' final day of fasting.

As was done the day before, they broke that day's fast at midday. For lunch, they had mixed vegetables and chicken laced with mayonnaise and ketchup. That was eaten with gusto as they shared what God had done for them during the previous days of fasting. Later, they drank some Pure Heaven non alcoholic wine and some pineapple as dessert.

Jimrince's childhood friend Christian, residing in the United States of America, later called him to enquire about him and Ellen his wife. He told Jimrince that they too were very much concerned, and before the conversation ended, he gave his friend Jimrince, a Western Union Transfer code for him to collect two hundred United States Dollars (200 USD) as his own contribution towards helping him and Ellen purchase some food items after the Lockdown because there were rumours that there would be a further Lockdown to contain the dreadful virus in the country.

At 5:00 pm, Jeredine, Ellen's close friend, called to tell her that she and her husband were to turn on the radio as a renowned man of God was going to prophesy to the nation at 6:00pm that day. At 6:00 pm, Jimrince and Ellen decided to come out of their flat, to observe what was going on, they noticed that their neighbours had equally come out to respond to the prophetic word of God. Everybody had a radio and had to listen and follow the instructions which the renowned man would give them on radio.

By 6:15 pm, there was a thunderous shout of "Jesus" and one would have thought that the Rapture had finally come. As if God heard the supplication of his children, the rainbow appeared in the sky. Ellen then remembered what happened in Noah's days after the flood and she became convinced that God was pleased with the nation. A moment of jubilation followed the shout and the solemn atmosphere suddenly changed.

There was not much done after that prophecy and shout, and when finally Mr. and Mrs. Ota retired to bed that night, they heaved a sigh of relief because they had come to the conclusion that the worst days were over and that better days were ahead. When they finally slept, they snored and it sounded like that of a train which was approaching a steep hill.

Emancipated

The Anglican Cathedral in Sealtown located in the heart of the Central Business District of Leone Town was jam-packed that Saturday morning as dignitaries from all walks of life marched through the entrance to take their respective seats before the start of the nuptial ceremony between Pearlmira Kentuckey and Jim Wotah. As it was a very classical wedding, a good number of the invited ladies wore expensive "ready-made" dresses and hats that matched their shoes and bags. The men also did not want to be left out of the show of wealth as they complemented the ladies by putting on expensive silk suits and high quality designer shirts that matched their leather shoes. Some even went the extra mile and wore high quality top hats.

Indeed it was a great day for Pearlmira who had thought that she would never get married. She was from a very modest family whose religious life was untainted. The family of four – father, mother, brother and Pearlmira - had their fervent hope and trust in God.

They never undertook any project without praying and fasting. They tried as best as possible to live at peace with their neighbours and as Mrs. Canishia Kentuckey was a midwife, she helped those underprivileged pregnant women who did not have the means to pay the necessary admission fees in the existing maternity homes when they were in labour. Even though their only daughter – Pearlmira – was still unmarried at age 39, they believed fervently that though the marriage of their daughter might tarry, it would surely come to pass.

At 11:45 am, Mr. Edward Kentuckey was at the entrance of the church with his daughter on his left hand, waiting for the priest to announce the processional hymn. Mrs. Canishia Kentuckey and her son Eric had gone into the church to take their seats in the first row of the side reserved for the bride's parents. Other relatives were there gorgeously clad to support their niece Pearlmira. Jim's family was also well represented and the air of pomp and show of wealth from their own side were also visible; making the ceremony more exuberant.

When the hymn "Great is thy faithfulness, O God my father" was announced, Pearlmira felt her legs trembling and thought that an unexpected earthquake had taken place. In spite of this uneasy feeling, she had to face the reality by allowing her father to walk her down the aisle to meet her husband Jim. Her immaculate white bridal dress with diamond embroidery, specially ordered from France by the groom, glittered as they gracefully walked down the aisle. Her younger cousins Jeredine and Samuella had consented to be the bridesmaids at the wedding. They walked immediately behind Jeredine and Uncle Edward to see to it that the 72-inch train was attached to the bridal dress did not get hooked to any chair or object while they marched. Pearlmira was feeling a bit uneasy, yet she had to face reality and suppress her fear by smiling as she sang the processional hymn off-head. By the time they finished singing the final stanza of the hymn, she was already by the side of her handsome soon-to-be husband, Jim. Standing next to him, she was still in amazement as she had never thought that such a moment would ever arrive. She then remembered her school and university days which were full of very fond memories. She also remembered her friends who would discuss marriage issues when their lecturers did not show up for lectures.

One of them had predicted that Pearlmira would get married to a well-to-do man because she was very disciplined, serious, honest and optimistic. Years had passed and now it seemed that the prophecy of Jamestina was about to be realized because Jim was an affluent man. However, when Pearlmira had attended the wedding ceremony of the last of her friends about eight years ago, she thought that all was lost for her. That notwithstanding, one Friday night after the friend's wedding, while she was meditating on the word of God before saying her evening prayer, she heard a still small voice saying in unequivocal terms that she should just wait patiently and allow God to order her ways. Indeed, prophecy was really being fulfilled that Saturday 24th December.

The exchange of vows was the high point of the wedding. While Jim was bold and confident, Pearlmira was still nervous. She later realized that everything going on around her was real when the priest said:

"If anyone of you knows of any just cause or impediment why these two persons may not be lawfully joined in holy matrimony…"

There was great silence and her heart throbbed while they waited as it was the custom to observe a moment of silence at that point of the marriage. . After that silence, when no one raised any objection, the ceremony continued. At that time, Pearlmira had gained the desired confidence because she had been fully persuaded that she had been the only one Jim had been in love with. She wasted no time in repeating after the priest when it was time to exchange vows. Her exposure in Europe had had a positive effect on the way she expressed herself and one would imagine the cadence she spoke with. Jim too smiled graciously as he exchanged vows with his beloved wife.

When the priest asked "Who giveth this woman to be married to this man?" Mr. Edward Kentuckey walked majestically to hand over his dear daughter. While he did that, tears fell from his eyes but he managed to control them so that no one except his daughter and son-in-law would see it happen. Finally the bride and groom exchanged rings and the entire church was full of applause. The band of one of the famous secondary schools in that city played the fanfare.

When the fanfare was being played and her veil lifted by her husband, Pearlmira gave such a loud cry that everyone thought that something bad had happened to her. Yet it was tears of joy that she shed as her long awaited emancipation from being a spinster had come and here she was, after many years of waiting, married. While she cried, she remembered the night she first met Jim and he said he loved her. Being a naïve lady then, she turned down his offer on the pretext that she was still waiting for God's solution to her problem of getting a life-long partner. Jim did not insist much that evening but only asked for her telephone number which she gave reluctantly.

She finally became convinced that Jim was her real partner when the uninterrupted calls from him came in at least five times daily. At first, she thought that Jim wanted to get his way with her because of her outstanding beauty. Later, her perception changed and the competition between Jim and her started; if Jim called five times, she would make it six. In addition to that, she would send loads of text messages which ranged from the most religious to the most romantic. Three months after the proposal, both of them started visiting each other and that was closely followed by weekend dinners in the most luxurious restaurants and hotels in town, as well as parties with their colleagues and relatives. At six months of their courtship, the two had become so attached to each other that one would have likened them to Shakespeare's lovebirds Romeo and Juliet. They also took turns to collect one another from work. They were then nicknamed "the inseparables" by their friends.

Once, a lady in their church who did not like the relationship between Pearlmira and Jim, went and told Pearlmira that Jim was cheating on her and the only option was for her to quit the relationship. Pearlmira had almost done what the lady told her, but her mother Canishia noticed the sudden change in the relationship between her daughter and Jim. Being an experienced wife and mother, she summoned the two to a meeting and decided to enquire why the dramatic change had occurred. After a long discussion, she realized that her daughter was at fault and Canishia told her that she should apologize to Jim. She also counselled Pearlmira to be very cautious of the people who came around her as many of them might not want her to get someone handsome, intelligent and as kind as Jim. From that time on, she became very committed to Jim and would not allow anything to break their relationship.

When Pearlmira finished crying, her darling husband took his white handkerchief from his pocket to wipe her tears. That emotional scene left the congregation speechless. The silence was broken when the priest announced *"Love Divine all love excelling"* as the offertory hymn. As the wardens and sidesmen went around with their alms bags to collect the offering, one could see crispy notes of five and ten thousand leones coming from the purses and wallets of the worshippers.

After the nuptial prayers and benediction, the bride and groom were invited to sign the register. Unlike what was done in other churches, during weddings at the Cathedral, only those who were issued invitations to sign the register, were eligible to do so. While those eligible to sign the register walked to the altar, the band in attendance gave classical renditions to entertain the congregation. For a moment, Jim thought about his cousin's wedding three months earlier when he had been asked to sign. He felt so proud that day to sign his cousin's register. During that process, he longed for the day when he would be sitting and other people coming to sign his own wedding register. The day had finally arrived and he felt fulfilled as he watched not only the exquisite dresses of guests but also the different signatures of those invited to sign.

The solemnization ceremony was climaxed by the singing of the hymn "There shall be showers of *blessing*." That was preceded by a thunderous fanfare by the band.

As they sang while recessing, there were smiles of satisfaction on the faces of relatives and guests.

By the time they got to the west door of the church, there was someone standing there to put a crown and a sash containing different bank notes on Jim's head and Pearlmira's shoulders respectively. This was done due to the fact that Pearlmira was Branch Manager in one of the renowned banks and, as custom demanded, the bride and groom were to be decorated. The bride and groom were greeted with cheers from friends and relatives.

Taking a few steps forward, Jim and Pearlmira witnessed another drama: there were nurses who had come with their equipment and were calling on Dr. Jim Wotah to give urgent medical assistance. This was the norm for medical personnel when they got married and Jim, being a senior medical officer in the country, was not an exception. That drama also attracted the attention of a good number of the guests who initially did not understand why the nurses were standing by the entrance of the church with stethoscopes, surgical spirit, gauze and thermometers. The outcome of their drama was positive as those guests who were thrilled poured wads of bank notes to show their satisfaction.

The reception and party was to be held in the newly constructed five-star hotel along the beach. As they drove to the beach, the couple reminisced about their courtship days when they used to come to that beach on Sunday evenings to have quality time together.

Once, they were busy talking and having a good time when a thief came close by and pretended to be one of the cleaners in that area. Jim, who had some detective qualities, noticed the movement but did not raise any alarm as he wanted to know exactly what the "unannounced cleaner" wanted. He continued the conversation with his darling Pearlmira but kept an eye on the cleaner's movements. The latter had eyed Pearlmira's purse and as he stretched out his hand to snatch the purse, he was intercepted by Jim's hand. While he tried to escape, Jim had got up and had seized him. He was about to beat him up when the thief told him that someone had sent him to take the purse because he had tried all he could to get Pearlmira but nothing positive happened. When asked to show the person, Jim was astonished that his workmate, who always told him that he was lucky to have a beautiful lady like Pearlmira, was the culprit. Full of shame, Patrick asked Jim for forgiveness and vowed that he would never come close to Pearlmira. Jim also vowed that he would never have anything to do with Patrick as he was a back-stabber.

By the time they finished reminiscing, the couple was at the site where the incident had happened and all they did was to laugh their sides out. The distance between that point and the reception hall was short and Pearlmira graciously appealed to her husband Jim to come out of the car and walk the remaining distance. That request was immediately accepted by the husband and the entire entourage followed. One of Jim's uncles who had come from the United States of America to grace the wedding ceremony had also come with the famous bridal "Dollar Spray" which the bridesmaids carefully sprayed on the bride and groom while they walked to the entrance of the hall.

The reception was equally well-attended; the hall was gorgeously dressed with lilac and white, the designated colours of the day. The rich variety of food and drinks was another thing worth noting and guests could ask for anything they wanted from the French service which was used (l'apéritif, l' hors d'oeuvre, le plat principal, le dessert and le digestif). The waiters and waitresses were all smartly dressed and did their serving duty with commitment and dedication.

The cutting of the cake by the bride and groom was really stunning: a special stool had been designed for Dr. and Mrs. Jim Wotah to stand on and cut the base of the eleven-tier cake which was ordered by the bride's Aunty Tina from London. It was lilac-embroided with silver balls. It also had an artificial lighted fountain at the top and from a distance, one would think that it was the Eiffel Tower lit at night. The toasts and speeches alternated with the serving and everyone's favourite toast was that from the bridegroom. He was relaxed and at the same time outspoken when the speech was made. He also made some jokes where necessary to show his overwhelming joy. At the end of his speech he said:

"I have now got my missing rib which fits me as if its size had been measured before. I will love my wife and always protect her as long as we live on planet earth."

When it was her turn to give the vote of thanks, Pearlmira thought that she too should shower praises on Jim. Every sentence she made ended with "my darling husband" and everyone present clapped. She too ended her vote of thanks with these words:

"As of today, I am not living for myself but for my darling husband who has turned my mourning into laughter by leaving all the other beautiful ladies and choosing me to be his missing rib. I am now revealing the big secret to you our honoured guests. I am three weeks pregnant and please keep your ears to the ground because my darling husband Jim and I will definitely invite you all to the naming and christening ceremonies. I wish to express thanks to you all for coming and a million thanks to my darling husband for making me a complete woman today."

As if words were not enough, Pearlmira gently took her husband by the hand and gave him a wonderful hug and kiss when he finally stood up. That was the second time she did that to Jim. The first was at the party which followed her engagement, a week prior to the wedding. On that day, Jim had been sitting on the table prepared for him and his friends when Pearlmira came and told him that she wanted to say something to him in public. Little did Jim know that Pearlmira wanted to give him a public hug and kiss. When she did that, all present were pleased and they praised Pearlmira for being bold that night. The repetition of that act at the wedding reception also received the guests' approval.

When guests were asked to present their gifts, it was as if an international match had just ended and spectators were rushing to move out because every guest had a gift for the bride and groom. The chairman had to ask everyone to sit down and then called on the waiters and waitresses to ensure an orderly flow. As a sign of appreciation, souvenir items were handed to each guest who gave a present. One could hardly see the couple, for the number of gifts already received, covered the stage.

A party immediately followed the reception. As guests were earlier informed about the flow of events, rooms had been booked for those who might want to change from church to party attire. In view of this, thirty minutes was given to allow the change of clothes. The bride and groom also retired to the room which had been booked for their Honeymoon.

The party resumed in much higher spirits than during the reception. Some guests left at the end of the reception. Those who stayed on really had a good time. By 3 am, the hall was almost empty because most people were tired and had gone home for a short night's rest.

Jim and Pearlmira were also tired and decided to retire to their room. On the way out, they noticed a gentleman with "breasts". Curious to know who the individual was, they called one of the waiters to intercept him. That was swiftly done and when Jim got much closer, he asked the gentleman who he was. The latter told him that he was an invited guest. Jim knew he was lying and asked him who invited him. He said the bride's mother Mrs. Kamara had invited him. In Jim's annoyance, he grabbed the man by the shirt and as he did, canned drinks fell from his "breast". Jim then concluded that the gentleman must have sneaked in during the thirty minute interval when some guests left and others went to change. In his rage Jim said:

"How dare you. Don't you have a conscience? Think about those who were legally invited. They did not behave like you. In fact, my mother –in-law is not Mrs.

Kamara. People like you go to places unannounced and want to enjoy more than the invited guests."

With those words, he ordered the waiters to show the man the door. When that was done, he instructed them to take an inventory of all that was left and then moved to his room with his darling wife.

On entering the exquisitely prepared bedroom, Pearlmira noticed that her husband was angry, and to make him feel better, she hugged and tickled him. Soon, they forgot about the incident. Jim then turned on the television and both of them watched a Christmas Watchnight service in one of the cathedrals in England. They joyfully sang the carols and danced to the organ music as at one point in the service, the priest asked the organist to give an organ recital.

When they finally lay down, they continued singing until they fell asleep.

The following morning, which was Christmas day, they woke up a bit late but notwithstanding, they hurriedly got dressed to attend the traditional Christmas day service in Jim's church. Pearlmira was very excited to attend that service as it was obvious that the priest was going to welcome them as the newly wedded couple - a moment she had looked forward to for so long.

The Final Call

When Daisyclair arrived at the Coloto Clinic that Wednesday afternoon in May to see how her ailing husband was progressing, she least expected that she would see her son-in-law standing at the entrance. Her son-in-law's presence at the entrance of the hospital brought about some suspicion but she quickly dismissed pessimism which had almost preoccupied her thoughts.

Titus greeted his mother-in – law with a broad smile and even gave her a hug which was common between them. He then offered her a chicken sandwich which he had bought at the Crown Net Bakery. He then pulled her to the waiting room to sit and eat the food. When she was almost done with the eating, Titus went to his car and brought her a cold bottle of sprite which she slowly drank as they continued chatting. When Daisyclair finally finished eating, she got up from the bench with renewed energy and was about proceeding to the ward where her husband was admitted, when Titus, her son-in-law told her that Ekundayo, her husband was under the doctor's observation. He further told his mother-in-law that due to the doctor's observation of the patient (Ekundayo), visits to him had been restricted that day. Titus then brought out a prescription of medication, which according to him, was given by Doctor Kelfala and that they should buy them from one of the pharmacies down town. Daisyclair then told Titus that she had enough money and that she could rush to get the medication from the pharmacy they were referred to. Titus knowing that they need not buy any medication tried to convince her to get into his car as they could use his own money to buy the medication. After three minutes of tussle,

Daisyclair reluctantly climbed into Titus' car which was parked about five metres from the hospital. On their way, Titus thought of another plan and decided to tell another lie. This time, he told Daisyclair, his mother-in-law, that he would first of all like to see his wife Letticia who had earlier called requesting to see him. Daisyclair scolded Titus and told him that he could see Letticia after having bought the medication but with a smiling countenance, Titus pleaded with Daisyclair for them to make a two-minute stop at Letticia's before continuing their journey. Titus also mentioned that Letticia was at her grandmother's residence at Weston Road.

On the way to Bamidele's resident at Weston Road, Daisyclair became more and more uncomfortable and she engaged Titus in a conversation:

- *Titus, how is my husband doing? I hope nothing is wrong because you have refused me seeing him at the hospital and now, instead of taking me to the pharmacy to buy the prescribed medication, you are taking me to my mother's house where you claim your wife is waiting for you. Please, please, please, don't play any tricks on me!*

Still trying to be as calm as possible, Titus replied:

- *Mummy, as she was normally called, your husband is fine. Nothing is wrong with Dada Ekundayo. The only thing is that the doctor is strictly monitoring him and I believe that when he starts taking the medication, he will be fine.*

Daisyclair was still not satisfied and asked:

- *Why the monitoring Titus? When I left him this morning, Ekundayo was ok. We talked to each other and before leaving, he gave me the usual hug. So I am puzzled that he is being monitored by the doctor now.*

Still trying to evade the obvious answer which Daisyclair was seeking, Titus remarked:

- *Mummy, Dada Ekundayo was feeling hot and restless as there was blackout in the hospital. Consequently, the ward became hot and you know that as a result of his asthma, Dada Ekundayo started wheezing. Even though the windows were later opened, yet the ventilation was poor. At about 9:00 am, when Doctor Kelfala came in to do his usual rounds, he found dada Ekundayo sweating profusely. Curious to know why, doctor Kelfala ordered some tests to be conducted so that he could ascertain the cause of dada Ekundayo's profuse sweating. It could be that he is suffering from malaria which was not detected earlier and that may be the cause of his profuse perspiration coupled with the asthmatic attack.*

Daisyclair who had done some nursing course while she was in England with her husband Ekundayo, was shocked when she heard that her husband was sweating. Due to her nursing experience, when a sick person is sweating profusely other than suffering from malaria or related diseases, it was a sign of approaching death. After pondering over that statement from her son-in-law, she asked with a hint of rage:

- *I hope Ekundayo is not dead and you are pretending to me that he is still alive.*

Titus who was afraid but resolved not to let the cat out of the bag, confidently responded:

- *"No ma. How can he be dead? He is in the hospital. After purchasing the medication, both of us will return to the hospital and you will see your darling husband Ekundayo".*

With that response, Daisyclair felt temporarily relieved and gave a broad smile especially when her husband's name was mentioned.

The rest of the journey was done in silence and in two minutes, they arrived at Bamidele's residence. When Daisyclair got out of the car, she saw her sister Victoria, who she had left to take care of her husband at the hospital while she went to conduct the school exam that day. Seeing her sister aroused more curiosity as she wanted to know why Victoria was not at the hospital. Daisyclair recalled that before leaving to conduct the examination that morning, she had asked Victoria to wait for her in the hospital until she returned. Seeing her sister Victoria at their mother's house, Daisyclair came to terms with the reality and said:

"I know Ekundayo is dead. Please don't lie to me"

In order not to prolong the deception any further, Victoria burst into tears and confirmed the death of Ekundayo. From the entrance of the house to the living room, it was very difficult to control Daisyclair who had finally broken down in tears. Her daughter Letticia recommenced crying with her mother and neighbours had to rush into Bamidele's residence to know what was happening. The news was broken to them and they in return expressed their sympathy to Daisyclair and her daughter Letticia who were present then.

In this state of bewilderment, Daisyclair recalled what happened twenty-six years earlier when she got married to Ekundayo and had taken the solemn vow *for better or worse, till death do us part*. She had ever remained faithful to her husband since marriage and his death was a hard blow to her. She recalled the last Saturday in February that year when she got married to Ekundayo. Coming from an humble, religious but respected family, the wedding was well attended by her colleague teachers and friends of her social groups. Her father John, who was strict and time conscious was so much concerned that she got to church on time as he did not want to pay a fine to the church authorities should the bride be late. With so much joy and satisfaction that day, John willingly handed his daughter over to Ekundayo at the Catholic Cathedral which was packed full. After the wedding, the reception was held at their residence which had been well decorated by one of Daisyclair's cousins - Morpeh.

Daisyclair's elder sister Victoria had contacted a renowned caterer in town to prepare the food which was served. Her younger brother Cecil, who was working at the brewery, had got the drinks purchased at a discounted price. Ekundayo's aunty Dorothea who was a celebrated caterer did the three tier white and pink wedding cake which had currants, marzipan and other rich ingredients. Their mother Bamidele who was a seamstress of long standing did all the sewing for her younger daughters and the lilac lace embroided with pearl beads fitted them well.

Coming back to the reality, Daisyclair could not come to terms that her confidant, partner, husband, playmate, adviser and provider had changed time for eternity. She still imagined how cruel death was as its cold hands have separated her from her darling Ekundayo. When the sobbing ended, Daisyclair remembered that her two sons had not been informed about their father's death. Augustus who was a teacher in one of the boys' secondary schools in town and Andrew was a pupil in Junior Secondary School. In fact, Andrew had left home that fateful day with high hopes of visiting their father once he returned from school. Augustus had promised his father that when he returned from work that day, he would buy him bananas as his father Ekundayo loved eating them.

Fate had however struck and they could no longer see their loving dad who would buy biscuits, cakes and even soft drinks for them and their sisters everyday he returned from work. On Saturdays, he would take them to beach to have fun and relax after a hectic week. At the beach, Ekundayo and his family would have a very pleasant time. He would allow his children play on the sand and have fun, while he and Daisyclair would be discussing relevant issues pertaining to the welfare of the family. On other times, they would sit down and reminisce their childhood days, while their children played on the sand. Being a strict dad, he would not allow the children to swim because he would always recall the death of his elder brother Horatio who died by drowning years ago. Horatio's death was responsible for their mother's sudden death some thirty years ago because Horatio was her blue eye boy.

On Sundays, he would not allow anyone to do any other job than cooking rice. Being a staunch Christian, attending church service was a laid-down rule for everyone except if anyone was sick. He would normally say that if God had given all of them the desired strength to go to work and school during the week, why should his family be tired of going to God's house on Sundays to return thanks for the great benefits he had accorded them during the week? After church service, the family would return home, have lunch and take the usual Sunday nap. By 5 pm, they would watch movies and at 7 pm, the children were asked to complete their assignments or study until 8:30 pm which was normally bedtime for everyone.

Daisyclair also hailed from a strong religious family and her father who was Lay Reader in church was very particular about seeing darling his wife and children attend church service. Before her marriage to Ekundayo, attending church service was one of the criteria Daisyclair and her siblings had to fulfil should they want to visit their friends or any other relative on Sundays. The other things they as children had to fulfil were to complete all the household chores and buy things from the market before Sunday as no work, other than sweeping the house and cooking rice, was done in their house on Sundays.

Back in the sitting room at Bamidele's residence, Letticia, who had found the telephone number of Augustus' boss in her diary, decided to call the principal to inform him about the death of their dad, and to ask that Augustus be released that day. When the principal received the phone call, he was shocked because he had known Ekundayo in the area he lived when he was young. He promised Letticia that he would do as she had requested.

Augustus was teaching that morning when the principal sent to call him. It was very unusual for the principal to send for him especially when he was teaching. As a result of this, Augustus felt very uneasy. When he got to the principal's office, he was asked to give a summary of the number of classes he had to teach. Even when Augustus told him that he had to teach till the end of the school day, the principal insisted that he should abandon his classes and rush home and collect a letter for him from his mother Daisyclair. At first, Augustus was surprised that his principal, who was very stern, was telling him to abandon teaching that day in order to run an errand for him. Mr. Pee was one such principal who never tolerated indolence among his staff and telling Augustus to abandon teaching that day, was really surprising to Augustus.

When Augustus reached their home at Rook Lane, he was stunned to see his aunty Esther and other relatives looking at him with consternation. Meanwhile, his mother was still at Bamidele's residence. After the normal greetings, aunty Esther burst out crying. Augustus realized that something was wrong and upon further enquiring, he was told that his father had passed on. The first thing he did was to inform neighbours in Rook Lane and then went to his grandmother's house to meet his mother. When he arrived at his grandmother's, the crying session restarted and for twenty minutes, no one could control Augustus and his mother and sibling Letticia. After that show of passion, Augustus left and decided to go back home to put the house in order for sympathizers who were bound to start coming to visit his mum Daisyclair when she returned to the house at Rook Lane.

At 4:00 pm, while he was cleaning the house, Augustus saw his younger brother Andrew who had returned from school. Knowing that Andrew was his dad's favourite, Augustus was afraid to reveal the death news. Instead, he told Andrew that their mummy wanted to see him at their grandmother's residence.

By 6:30 pm, Daisyclair had returned to her home at Rook Lane and she was greeted by a number of sympathizers who had come to console her. Being a senior teacher in one of the private primary schools in town, Daisyclair had been a mother and source of help to many children and parents especially when some of the parents could not meet the demands the school was levying on them. She would either stand as a guarantor or pay the charges in order to alleviate the pressure on the parents. Therefore, when they learnt that she had lost her husband, they spread the news to one another like wild fire. It was in the state of solemnity and grief that Ekundayo's elder brother Ernest and cousins, Cyril and Mary, came to sympathize. Since Ekundayo fell ill, his elder brother Ernest neither visited him in the hospital nor did he send anything financial support to cushion the expenses which Daisyclair was undergoing. Mary was the cousin who had insulted Daisyclair on the day of her marriage to Ekundayo. At that time, she had wanted his cousin Ekundayo to get married to her friend Francess but Ekundayo did not accept that proposal and went ahead and married Daisyclair. In the state of disappointment, Mary had vowed to make Daisyclair uncomfortable in her matrimonial home and here she was to create panic for Daisyclair. Cyril was their maternal cousin who lived in Canada and had lost communication with his cousin Ekundayo for more than a decade. He was on holidays when his cousin died and decided to accompany the others to express sympathy.

When the three arrived at the residence, they greeted Daisyclair who replied to them in a polite manner. After five minutes, they started insulting Daisyclair and even accused her of killing their cousin Ekundayo. While Daisyclair was baffled at their behaviour, her son Augustus stood up and told them the truth in their face. Other sympathizers condemned their behaviour and being ashamed of themselves, Ernest, Cyril and Mary told Daisyclair that they would not contribute a cent to the funeral expenses of their relative. Being resolute, Daisyclair retorted and told them that she cared less whether they contributed to her husband's funeral or not. She further told them that the husband would be buried with the pomp he deserved and they would see and wonder. When the trouble makers left, sympathizers who were present decided to console Daisyclair afresh and admonished her not to be worried as God would supply all what she needed for the burial of her husband.

The following morning was very hectic as Daisyclair and her children had to run so many errands. Letticia decided to go to the City Council to arrange for the grave where her father would be laid to rest. Augustus had to first accompany his mother to the funeral home to choose the casket they would give to the late man and after that, to town to purchase white lace window curtains and the mourning attire for the family. It was a custom that Krios normally wore black as mourning garb when a husband or father or even a mother died. However, Daisyclair had to change the rule as she did not like wearing black. She finally decided to choose navy blue with a shade which was much nearer to black. Much later that day, Letticia went to the various radio stations and paid for the obituary announcements so that those who were yet to hear about Ekundayo's demise, would hear should they listen to the obituary announcements.

The Dean of the cathedral as well as other priests in the church visited them in the evening and conducted a short evensong for the family. Daisyclair was very much appreciative of that gesture and thanked them for their kind thought. Before leaving, a purse was handed over to Daisyclair in recognition of Ekundayo's strong financial commitment to the cathedral while he was alive.

The days following the death were full of activities as every little arrangement had to be completed before Ekundayo's internment. The visits by sympathizers both near and distant were regular. There were prayer sessions every evening at the residence as it was the norm in their family circle. During those prayer sessions, they interceded for God's provision, comfort and courage for the family to face the ultimate day which would be the final parting.

The family had decided to hold a vigil at their residence on the day before the funeral. As Augustus and Andrew were choristers at the Cathedral, the choir was obliged to attend and pay homage to the family as was the tradition.

The vigil was scheduled for 7:00 pm and at 6:45 pm, the house was packed full with mourners. Daisyclair sat in one corner in the sitting room flanked by her three children, while the choir had to contend with the little space on the other side. Scripture readings and tributes were all done but the tribute of the evening was that which Augustus did. It was so emotional that most of the mourners shed tears. Augustus told mourners how caring their dad was and the way he remained faithful to their mother in spite of all the goings-on in their area. At the end, he quoted from one of the plays of William Shakespeare and another quote was from John Dryden's poem. When the vigil ended, light refreshment was served and mourners ate in a solemn atmosphere. When all of the mourners had left, Augustus, his brother Andrew and his cousins decided to change the curtains and do the final touch for the final departure of a beloved dad.

On Friday 27th May, the family had got up a little earlier than they did on other days. After the usual family prayers, Andrew and his friends, who had come to assist the family, arranged the chairs and meticulously cleaned the entire house and compound. Daisyclair was urged by her mother and sister to take an early bath and get dressed as she was the focal point that day. When she finally got dressed, she was forced to have some food even though she protested that she was not hungry. By 10:30 am, Daisyclair's brothers had come to the residence to collect Augustus as he was the one who was to collect his father's remains from the funeral home. Augustus tried to dodge that duty but was prevailed upon by his maternal uncles.

At the funeral home, Augustus broke down in tears when he saw his father lying speechless in an exquisite mahogany trellis casket embroidered with blue and white cloth. Ekundayo was dressed in a sky blue suit and white shirt with a floral neck tie which his best friend Paul had given Daisyclair to put on him. Augustus' uncles could not help but cry as they reflected how Ekundayo had been a loving brother-in-law to them and would always go the extra mile to satisfy their financial and material needs. After the modalities at the funeral home had been done, the corpse was released and in a motorcade, Augustus and his uncles, who had come with their cars, drove solemnly to the residence at Rook Lane.

When the funeral van alighted at the residence, Daisyclair was the first to run to the gate as if she was going to grab her husband. Fortunately, some young men who were around saw her rushing and they in turn rushed at her to prevent her from doing anything irrational. She was then brought to the living room where the laying out of the corpse for viewing was to be done. After prayers were offered, the funeral home attendants open the casket for viewing. Daisyclair could not contain herself when she saw her husband lying lifeless. In fact she fainted and fortunately for the family, there was cousin Olu, who was a medical personnel, was around. He did his best to resuscitate his cousin Daisyclair in order not to have another disaster. During that time, the children had become so much worried as they did not want to have another death like it happened some years ago when the wife of a distant relation died on the day her husband was laid out for viewing.

When Daisyclair finally regained consciousness, she asked her son Andrew to put a chair next to the casket so that she could sit and sing parting songs for her husband.

Her wish was granted but was strictly monitored by her brothers and children so that there would not by any recurrence of collapse. At one point she ordered her sons to put off the musical set which was playing solemn music and allow her to sing for her husband.

Gradually, the time for the church service drew nigh. At 2:45 pm, the Dean of the Cathedral came to view the corpse and at the same time said the farewell prayer before the closure of the casket. The Dean of the Cathedral was very much moved when he saw his pupil Ekundayo lying motionless in a casket. As a pupil at the Grammar School while he was principal, he remembered Ekundayo being brilliant and studious and his name was always among the best pupils who received prizes during speech day and prize giving ceremonies, organized by the school. He also remembered when Ekundayo got married to Daisyclair twenty-six years ago; Daisyclair's father was his schoolmate and he had been Ekundayo's principal; so he was one of the clergy men who solemnized the marriage between Ekundayo and Daisyclair.

When he finished praying, the entire parlour went noisy as Daisyclair, her children and other relatives were bidding Ekundayo farewell with endless tears. The scene was really painful and scary and it was really difficult to control the emotions of the children and their mother as they could not help but cry. In fact, Daisyclair clung tenaciously to the casket that it was difficult for the funeral home attendants to close the casket. When they finally removed her hands from the casket, the attendants hurriedly closed the casket and Daisyclair was only left shouting the following phrase: *Good bye my husband, good bye my friend and confidant, good bye the father of my children."* The casket was then put in the funeral van and the cortege left for the church. As Ekundayo's death was sudden, the walk to the church was very solemn. Some neighbours who had been impacted by his kindness while he was alive, could not help but cry while walking. At one point, Sarah, the dedicated family maid fainted. Fortunately, there were some men walking beside her. They quickly held her to prevent her from hitting her head on the floor. She was pulled aside and taken to the nearest house where they tried to resuscitate her.

By the time they cortege arrived at the church, it was packed full of mourners. Being a renowned teacher, Daisyclair's friends as well as parents had come to pay their last respect to her husband Ekundayo. Ekundayo's workmates were there in full attendance as he was also a prominent accountant in a reputable organization. The choir of the cathedral was also present to do the final service to the father of two choristers: Augustus and Andrew. The Dean of the Cathedral's homily was taken from Hebrews 9:27. He also gave a wonderful biography of Ekundayo making reference to Ekundayo's school days while he served as principal at the Grammar school; the school Ekundayo attended. The rest of the requiem mass went as planned. When the withdrawal hymn *"Sing Alleluia in Duteous Praise"* was announced, Daisyclair again burst into uncontrollable sobbing with tears falling like beads from her eyes. She was comforted by her son Augustus and daughter Letticia. Supported on both sides by her children, she marched right behind the casket after the priests had recessed. All she could say was *it is well; this is the "Endless Alleluia"*

Arriving at the west door of the church, Augustus friends were already there to take the casket to the funeral van. One of them, Mark, was in tears also. He remembered how generous uncle Ekundayo was to him especially when he was in school. He recalled when uncle Ekundayo, as he called Augustus' father, paid his fees for two consecutive years when his own parents were unable to do so as a result of his father's redundancy from the institution he was working at. Had it not been for uncle Ekundayo's timely intervention then, he would not have become a prominent lawyer in society.

As they processed to the cemetery, mourners sang solemn hymns and Negro Spiritual songs. The most captivating of Negro Spiritual songs was the one titled *"my brother where you're going to, I am going to the Lord."* That song brought assurance to Daisyclair who was confident that her husband died knowing and serving the Lord Jesus Christ with his resources. Four years earlier, Ekundayo and Daisyclair had surrendered everything to God by being Born Again. As Born Again Christians then, Ekundayo and Daisyclair decided to serve the Lord with their resources, both physical and financial. Apart from attending services at the Cathedral, they would never miss mid-week services at the Holy Fire Pentecostal Church which was their second church. On second and fourth Sundays, they would attend morning services at the church together with their children and would feel the impact of both prayer sessions and the preaching. In fact, when the church was doing a renovation, Ekundayo and Daisyclair did not only give their financial support but were present every Saturday morning to lend their hand: Daisyclair would join the ladies to prepare food for the workers while Ekundayo was with the men to fetch water to do the concrete.

Back in the funeral van, Daisyclair recalled those precious moments which had been marred by death. She too was singing the song as it was Ekundayo's best Negro spiritual and one could see her broad smile as she sang in anticipation of her husband's going to heaven.

At 5:15pm, the cortege arrived at the cemetery. In contrast to the smiles in the funeral van, Daisyclair's eyes had become like grapes and were full of tears. The cemetery was the final parting point and she just did not know what to do. If she had the power to bring Ekundayo back to life, she could have done that but as a result of her inability to do that, she had the only option to face the reality which was her husband had gone to eternity. From the entrance of the cemetery to the graveside, the priests recited biblical verses. While supported by her daughter and sons, Daisyclair could only be heard faintly saying *"at last the end is real; my husband, brother, confident and father of my children."*

She managed to do the committal and after the committal and prayers, Daisyclair slowly paced forward as if she wanted to throw herself into the gaping grave. When Augustus saw that, he quickly grabbed his mother and pulled her to the side where his uncle Cecil was standing. His uncle Cecil immediately got hold of her and took her straight to his car which was parked nearby. Letticia and Andrew were also asked to follow their mum home. When the car drove off, Augustus returned to his father's grave and monitored the grave diggers while they hastily cover the grave with Mother Earth. When that ended, he was taken home by his other uncle Christian.

Back in the house, there was a large crowd which had come for the refreshment as was the norm. While Daisyclair was wondering how the number of mourners had increased and at the same time finding a way to weed out the crashers, she heard a whisper from her sister Hannah that she should just forget about the crowd and allow everyone to be served. As was the norm, an elderly relative was asked to say prayers before the refreshment was served. There was a lot of food and drinks to serve; as a result of Daisyclair's generosity in the community and to relatives and friends, they had brought a lot of food and drinks to show their appreciation to Daisyclair and family. When everyone was satisfied, Daisyclair told one of her children to ask those serving to prepare take-away packages for those who were still around. This was done to avoid food wastage. As the packs were delivered to everyone present, there was some kind of satisfaction and gratitude on the faces of mourners.

When everyone had gone home, Daisyclair summoned her children to a family meeting. At the meeting, she admonished them to stay united in spite of the fact that their father was no longer alive. She furthered that they should always maintain the prestige that the family had lived up to and for no reason should they allow themselves to be shamed or defeated. When she ended speaking, the children pledged that they would always maintain the values which had been inculcated in them.

At 10:00 pm, Daisyclair had a phone call from a close friend of hers who expressed shock at the demise of Ekundayo. She was about asking about the date of the funeral when Daisyclair interrupted and told her that they had buried him that day. Sarah could not believe her ears and told her friend that she was coming instantly to see Daisyclair and her family. Within forty-five minutes, she was at Daisyclair's with her husband Tom. Seeing her friend, she rushed and hugged her and another round of tears and sobbing followed. During her sobbing, she narrated how much concern Ekundayo had shown in order to see that her marriage was successful. Tom, who was not very emotional like his wife, hugged Daisyclair and told her that all was not lost as he and his family would always be ready to give whatever assistance to Daisyclair's family. Daisyclair was lost for words at the show of kindness. She told her son Augustus to get some food and drinks for aunty Sarah and Uncle Tom. After eating, they started reminiscing the golden days they spent together as friends. Little did they know that time was far spent. By the time they realized it, it was half past one and being worried about the safety of her friend and husband, Daisyclair encouraged them not to return to their house until the following morning. For that reason, she ordered her son Augustus to make his room available for the visitors. In ten minutes, the room was ready and before everyone went to bed, Tom requested that they had a family devotion. That was very solemnly and when Tom prayed, his voice faltered. Everyone retired to bed after that devotion and within a short time, a graveyard silence was noticed in the house.

Moving On

When Cornelius received news from the Head of Administration that he should relocate to another flat within 72 hours, he just could not believe his ears. After having served his institution for more than a decade, he felt that it was rather unfair on the part of the administration to take a rather hasty decision without considering his status in the organization. In spite of the short notice, Cornelius felt good that he would be relocating but that did not make him lose sight of the imminent hassle he would have to go through in the relocation process.

He then remembered the similar hassle he went through some twelve years ago when he first relocated from his parents house to an accommodation which the office had offered him. At that time, his former boss called him and after a wonderful discussion, he told Cornelius that having worked for two years with great satisfaction for his organization, he was going to offer him a two-bedroom flat in order to help him solve the constraints he was having with transportation. Upon hearing this, Cornelius was pleased because at that time, he was still single and was staying with his parents in a very comfortable house which his father had built. He thought that relocating would give him the opportunity to be more independent. Because living in his parents' house, he was not very worried about acquiring his own furniture and other cooking equipment. All his earnings were saved at the bank because his parents did not ask him to contribute anything towards the welfare of the home. For them, Cornelius was still a child irrespective of the fact that he was working.

He still remembered that day, twelve years earlier, when he was offered his first accommodation and how confused he was: at that time, Cornelius' first thought was to reject the offer as he was not willing to leave his parents who had showered him with so much love and care even when he was in the working class. However, one night, while he was discussing the issue with his fiancée Alison, who was working in a banking institution, she convinced him to accept the offer. Even though it was very difficult to succumb to the wish of his fiancée, he finally accepted and started the preparations without telling his parents. Three days later, when they were having dinner, he broke the news to his parents. His mother was very shocked and wanted to know the reason:

-    Cornelius, what have we done to you? [1]

-    "Mummy, you have not done anything to me. You and dad have been very great to me and I wonder what the world would have been like without you as parents".

-    "Then what has come over you to tell us that you want to leave us? You know that being here with us, we have the best company ever. After all, we have nurtured you from infancy and now you have grown up to adulthood and are our treasure."

-    "Mama, I think that I should move on and my stay with you will not allow me become independent. I know how much love and care you have showered and are now showering on me but I believe that, if I move out to stay on my own, I will be independent and acquire my own furniture. You know that I am to marry Alison in a few months and when I get a flat on my own, we can manage our own problems and where there is difficulty, we can call on you for advice."

"So does it mean that your father and I do not have the resources anymore to help you?"

"No mama. You have all the power to help me. With all the property and wealth that have been bestowed on me, I am very much mindful of your support to me. The reason is that I just want to know how independence means".

- "Then if that is your decision, I wish you all the best in your plans."

When the conversation ended, they continued the dinner in silence. As there was not more to discuss, Cornelius said good night to his parents and went to his bedroom. Ten minutes later, a knock was heard on his door and when he opened it, he saw his father. He welcomed him to his room as it had been more than three months since Jonathan, the father, had entered his son's room. For him, Cornelius should have his privacy irrespective of the fact that he was still staying with them. Unlike Jonathan, Modupeh, the mother would just knock and, without waiting for an answer, she would just turn the knob and enter. Of course she knew that her son was well-reared and would not expect any wayward friend in the room. But she had been used to it and when questioned by her husband, she replied that "no matter how tall the okra tree is, it will never be taller than its owner"

When Jonathan had sat down on a chair near Cornelius' bed, he said:

- "Son, I know your feelings and your views about being independent. However, I want to caution you to be extra careful about those who gather [2] around you. Some may come because of your success. Others because you are generous, while others still will come around just to know your future plans and intentions[3]. In all these, don't forget to pray. You know how devoted we have been to prayer. Don't forget that in everything God should take pre-eminence."

With tears falling down his cheeks, Cornelius replied:

"Daddy, I will never disappoint you. I know how much mummy and you have invested in me to make me what I am today. Rest assured that wherever I may find myself, this family name will not be likened with shame and regret and I assure that you will get the feedback.[4]"

Jonathan then put his hand on Cornelius' shoulder for a moment and when the sobbing ended, he left to meet his wife in their bedroom.

The following day, Cornelius went to see Alison and explained all that had happened. She was happy for him and when they had finished their discussion, both of them left Alison's office to finalize the arrangements for moving into the new accommodation.

On November 15th that year, Cornelius finally said goodbye to his parents. The departure was very emotional but was expedient. His parents were still not convinced about him being safe in his new accommodation. In view of that, they decided to accompany him. Upon arrival at the house, they noticed that it was an ideal place with two bedrooms, a spacious parlour and dining room, a well arranged kitchen and a store and garage. As devout Christians, the parents insisted to say prayers and dedicate the house. When that was done, they stayed another hour before leaving. For the first time in years, Cornelius had to sleep away from home.

Coming back to the present Cornelius decided to go and have a chat with the head of administration who had informed him to move to his new flat in 72 hours. Unfortunately, he did not meet Mr. Browne and was obliged to return to his office to continue his work. Back in his office, Cornelius could not do anything much except for a few emails he sent to some business partners.

When the person knocking at his door finally entered the office, Cornelius noticed that it was his messenger who had brought in some mails from the reception. After receiving the correspondences from his assigned messenger, he managed to do a few reports as the company's Annual General Meeting was to be held in two weeks. When he finished the final report, he decided to check if Mr. Browne had returned to his office. At Mr. Browne's office, he told him that he wanted to enquire why he was given only 72 hours to relocate. Full of smiles, Mr. Browne remarked:

-       "Mr. Cole, I know how you feel at this moment because as Manager of the Public Relations Department in this Import and Export Business organization,[5] we should have informed you much earlier. You may agree with me that our organization is one that recognizes hard work of its staff. You have been very dedicated to duty and for the number of years you have served in this organization, you have earned a lot of success. At the same time, you have made this organization one of repute. We in the administration had a closed door meeting and everyone agreed that you had done a lot for the organization. As a result of that, we decided that you occupy an apartment in the newly constructed three storey building at Regent. This apartment has a master bedroom and two other bedrooms, a spacious parlour, a well equipped kitchen and a garage for two cars. This offer is commensurate to your position and I believe that you will like it."

"In addition, your new flat is close to the beach which adds more to the comfort. This is all I have to say for now. Do you have anything to say sir?"

"I am lost for words sir. I never knew that I was appreciated by the administration. Thanks so much for the offer and I would like to say I am grateful."

"Never mind Mr. Cole. Considering the fact that you may have to put yourself in order before moving in to the new flat, the Administration has also been gracious to allow you move in at your own convenience. We have realized that you are a very key player in this organization and we must not treat you in any unfit manner. Thanks so much and I hope you will contribute more to the organization."

With those words, Cornelius left the Mr. Browne's office that bright and sunny afternoon, very pleased. When he finally returned to his office, he shut the door and offered a prayer of thanksgiving to the God of Israel as he had been taught by his parents since he was a young boy. After that, he called his father to announce the news to him. His father was so pleased to learn that his son was appreciated by a very renowned organization in the country. He told him that history was repeating as it was the same way he was honoured while he was working as Marketing Manager for a renowned Business Organization some twenty years ago.

Cornelius also recalled that incident as was in secondary school then. He remembered that day when his father came home from work and announced to his family that they were to relocate to a much bigger apartment which the organization had rented for him. At first, Mrs. Cole was annoyed because for her, where they lived was much closer to the school where she taught, and moving to another location which was two kilometres away was not to her advantage. Cornelius was preoccupied about losing his school friends especially those who were in the same study group as he was. However, after much persuasion by his wife, even though she too was disadvantaged,[6] Mr. Jonathan Cole was able to move into the new flat and within a short time his wife and son had got themselves adjusted to the new environment.

Coming to the present, Cornelius decided to visit his parents after work that day. Upon arrival, he met his parents as usual in the living room. His father who had informed his wife about Cornelius' offer, following the telephone conversation earlier, gave Cornelius a hug. Mrs. Cole, Cornelius' mother, expressed happiness upon hearing her son's success story and the reward his organization was giving him. Before he left his parents' house, his mother Modupeh insisted that Cornelius have dinner with them. That offer was graciously accepted and during dinner, all three of them chatted well and discussed current as well as past issues. When dinner ended, Cornelius went home.

The following morning, he called his fiancée Alison to reveal the good news and she was filled with so much delight that her fiancé was appreciated by his bosses.

As the days went by, Cornelius had to do a lot of errands as a way of getting himself ready for the new apartment. In fact, he decided to change his entire furniture in the new apartment and as he was led by the spirit of God, he decided that his messenger Pa Santigie should be the beneficiary of the old furniture. He knew that the gift would come as a surprise to Pa Santigie who had been very respectful to his boss. Cornelius also considered how faithful and dedicated Pa Santigie had been to him. Even though Pa Santigie was older than he was, yet he showed his boss the maximum respect and devotion any junior worker would have done to his boss. He was always willing to run errands for Cornelius who in turn would ask him to keep the change for himself should there be any left after running the errands.

At midday, Pa Santigie came to his boss to check whether he wanted to send him on an errand. Cornelius nodded as usual and gave Pa Santigie some money for him[7] to buy food at the restaurant which was about one hundred yards away from the office. When he returned, he handed the food to his boss as he usually did and Cornelius asked him to sit down. Pa Santigie was worried and asked his boss what the matter was.

Pa Santigie, you have done me no harm. It is just that I would like to know how big is your parlour.

"My boss, you know that I live in a one-bedroom flat with my wife and a son."

"Well I have decided that all my furniture in the old house will go to you as a way of showing how much I appreciate you."

Full of surprise, Pa Santigie could just only say thanks to his boss. He also offered prayers for God's protection and direction and, when he finished,[8] Cornelius said thanks for the gesture. He further informed him that he should collect the items in a week.

When Pa Santigie left the office, he went to inform his friends about what had happened between his boss and him. Everyone was happy for him and encouraged him to continue being faithful.

A week later, Pa Santigie collected his gift and that coincided with Cornelius' moving into his new house. To show how generous Cornelius was, he decided to rent a delivery van for him as Pa Santigie was financially unable to do so.

The following morning, Cornelius woke up feeling fresh and fulfilled, having overcome the hassle of moving into the new apartment. As everything was in a torpsy turvy state, he ordered his breakfast from the nearby restaurant. When the food was finally delivered, Cornelius ate in haste as he did not want to be late for work. When he arrived in the office, he was told by the General Manager that a visiting guest would like to have a meeting with him as the guest was also involved in public relations. The meeting was scheduled to take place in the conference room at 11:00 that day. Being told about the meeting, Cornelius finished the work which was on his table so that on his return from the meeting, he would not be overworked.

As scheduled, the meeting started at 11:00 am and the head of administration presided over that meeting. Mr. Toulouse, the guest, was introduced and was later asked to make a presentation. He was a tall, slim and handsome black American in his mid fifties. He was equally full of smiles and was very friendly. At the meeting, he told members present about the way the import and export business had grown worldwide.

In addition, he expressed satisfaction at the fact that Cornelius' business organization had a high repute in

America. He further shared some tips on how to make the business grow in spite of growing challenges. When he finished his twenty-minute presentation, there was a round of questions and answers followed.[9] Cornelius became popular during the questions and answers session as he was one who asked most of the questions. Noticing how brilliantly Cornelius asked questions, Mr. Toulouse later asked him to join him for dinner at 6:00 that evening at his hotel which was not too far from the office.

Having lived in the West for some time with his parents, Cornelius knew that time was of the essence and was at the *Mon Amour* hotel reception at five minutes to six. Mr. Toulouse later joined him at the reception and they gracefully walked to the restaurant. As a five-star hotel, the restaurant served mouth watering cuisine. Being a modest individual, Cornelius ordered for something simple. Mr. Toulouse who was visiting Africa for the first time decided to have a taste of one of the African dishes on the menu. While eating, Mr. Toulouse explained how he had to overcome a number of challenges in order to succeed in life, given that his father died when he was ten years-old and the onus was on his mother who had to take care of four children. As a teacher, she instilled in her children honesty, hard work and resilience. He intimated that all of them turned out as successful individuals and they were taking great care of their mum.

Cornelius also narrated part of his success story to Mr. Toulouse, and quite apart from the fact that he was the only child to his parents, they did not pet him. Rather, he was given the right type of upbringing. He told Mr. Toulouse that had it not been for the organization that had offered him accommodation twice, he would have still stayed with his parents. When he said that, Mr. Toulouse chuckled and told him that he was lucky to have both parents alive.

By the time the seeming unending conversation finally ended, the waiter was at their table with the bill. As it was Mr. Toulouse who had invited Cornelius, he used his credit card to pay. When they finally left the restaurant, it was very dark and, as a sign of respect, Mr. Toulouse accompanied his guest to his car and bade him a nice good evening.

The following day, news had spread in Cornelius' office about his brilliant performance the previous day. His boss was very pleased and called him to his office to congratulate him. When he entered the General Manager's office, he was given a seat.[10] His boss, who had previously been very stern towards him, was just relaxed and asked:

- *How did you feel, Mr. Cole, in interacting with an international expert?*

- *Sir, I felt good. I would first of all want to express thanks and appreciation for allowing me to be part of that discussion. In addition, you know that I am a man who does a lot of research and*

---

as such, I was very much au fait with most of what was discussed during our meeting.

- *"I know that Mr. Cole"*[11] was the General Manager's reply. *I know how much you have done and sacrificed just to project the organization's image and I am confident that you will do more.*

- Thanks so much, sir, for the compliment. By the grace of God Almighty, I assure you that I will always project the organization's image.

Having said that, he said goodbye to his boss and returned to his office. Cornelius spent the rest of the day sending communiqués and other related correspondences to partners. At a quarter to five, his phone rang and when he received the call, it was Mr. Toulouse who called to express thanks to Cornelius for making it to the dinner the previous day. As a way of reciprocating, Cornelius gave Mr. Toulouse an advance invitation to a lunch the following Sunday in his apartment. Mr. Toulouse accepted .

When Cornelius returned home that evening, he called his parents to inform them about Mr. Toulouse visit the following Sunday and told them that were we also invited. When Alison visited him that evening, Cornelius explained how he was commended by the General Manager for his brilliant performance the previous day and made mention of the invitation he had given to Mr. Toulouse to have lunch with them. Alison, who was a methodical and disciplined lady like Cornelius, decided that they should make the list of the items they would need to prepare on that day. When that was finalized, Alison told Cornelius that she would pay part of the expenses because the honour Cornelius had was hers too. At first Cornelius objected but when he saw that Alison was insisting, he consented. During dinner, they discussed how they had spent their day after which, Alison asked her fiancé to accompany her to her house.

As planned, on the Saturday before the proposed lunch, Cornelius went to pick up Alison to go shopping. They decided to start at Choicest Supermarket on Kenson Road which was one of the top supermarkets in that area. Upon entering the supermarket, Alison noticed a childhood friend in one of the corners. Joanna was happy to see her friend and, in the two minuets they engaged in a chat, Alison learnt that her friend was working for the United Nations in Kigali but had come home to attend the funeral of her great grandmother who died at age 97. The both exchanged contact numbers and promised to continue the dialogue through social media. When she joined Cornelius, they went to the dairy products freezer and bough some ham, chicken and the famous Camembert cheese which was considered one of the best types of cheese not only in France but also in their country. The other items including some white wine and other alcoholic and non alcoholic drinks were quickly selected from the shelves of the supermarket. Arriving at the cashier's, they had to wait for their turn.

On Saturdays, the supermarket was normally full because that is the time most people have the opportunity to do their shopping. Alison paid part of the bill while Cornelius paid the rest. Upon leaving the supermarket, they decided to make a stop at the local market to but some more beef products and vegetables as the vegetables sold outside the supermarket were fresher and tastier than those found in the supermarket. From the local market, they decided to have lunch in one of the Italian restaurants. Both Alison and Cornelius adored the famous *"Lasania"* dish which was made from pasta, cheese, minced meat and spices. Cornelius' love for this dish came when his father was working for an Italian Company in the United States of America; whenever they organized Christmas or Easter lunch, *"Lasania"* was always part of was among the delicacies prepared. For Alison, her delight in *"Lasania"* was as a result of her studies in Italy. As a student who wanted to economise her resources, she would always buy *"Lasania"* from the students' canteen.[12]

While eating that day, they recalled how much they enjoyed eating *"Lasagne."* At the end of the delicious meal, they left for Cornelius' house considering they had a lot of work to do. Alison had previously asked her younger sister Sarah to come over to help her with the preparations on that Saturday and, when they arrived at Cornelius', she was already there.

On Sunday morning, Cornelius did the final preparations before going to church and,[13] when he arrived, he went to sit with his parents who had arrived much earlier. At the end of the service, his mother suggested that they should go to their house before going over to Cornelius's for the lunch.

At 2:00 pm, Mr. Toulouse car was seen [14]moving up the drive. Cornelius who was already waiting for his guest went to the entrance to receive him. The warm embrace and convivial handshake assured Mr. Toulouse of pleasant company. He was then introduced to Mr and Mrs Cole and, forgetting about Cornelius who had invited him, Mr. Toulouse engaged in a fruitful conversation with Mr and Mrs Cole. Through the chat, Mr. Cole got to know that Mr. Toulouse and he had worked together in the United States of America; while he was Marketing Manager, Mr. Toulouse was in charge of publicity in the same department. Mr. Toulouse could hardly believe that he had met an old colleague after so many years. He then explained to Cornelius how hard-working and dedicated his father was; a man who was result-oriented. Mr. Toulouse concluded with this proverb *"like father like son"* and added that Cornelius was a true replica of his father in terms of intelligence, hard work and dedication to duty.

During lunch, the conversation continued and one could hear the cheerful laughter and jokes from a distance. In fact, Mr. Jonathan Cole asked his colleague Toulouse to give him his contact in order for them to keep in touch after the latter left for the United States on the following day. By 7:30 pm, the company broke up and everyone except Alison left. Alison, who had been the *head chef* during the lunch, was pleased that her would be in-laws were appreciated by Mr. Toulouse. She too left after cleaning up the kitchen and utensils used.

Three weeks later, Mr. Browne sent an urgent message that he would like to see Cornelius in his office. Baffled about what the urgent message was about, Cornelius decided to say a short prayer in his office. When he got to Mr. Browne's office, he was given a broad smile. He then told Cornelius that he had received a mail from Mr. Toulouse who had nominated Cornelius to present a paper at an International Conference on the Impact of Public Relations in the job market.[15] In addition, the conference, which would last for a week, would take place at the prestigious Hilton Hotel in San Jose, California. A per diem of 3,000 United States dollars would also be given him during that period. He heartily congratulated Cornelius and wished him success in the presentation. Before Cornelius left the office, Mr Browne told him to submit his passport to him by the following day so that he would do the administrative work on it.

The night before his departure, something unfortunate happened to him: thieves broke into Cornelius' apartment. Fortunately, he was not asleep; he was in the study finalizing his presentation for the conference in America. They had forced the back door of the house open and unfortunately for them, they hit one of the pots in the kitchen. That sound made Cornelius know that there were strangers in his house. He then shouted and the thieves, afraid that someone had noticed their movement, ran away. One of them ran out of luck and left his blue shirt in the kitchen.[16] Cornelius went to his bedroom to take his pistol as a defence should any of the thieves want to attack him. By the time he got to the kitchen, the thieves had run away. He saw the door wide open and a sky blue shirt on the floor. That shirt was worn by one of the thieves who had taken it off during their imminent operation and while running away, he was unable to collect it. Cornelius called one of the night guards and when he questioned him on how the thieves gained access to his apartment while he was on duty, the guard replied that he was not aware of any intruder. Picking up the blue shirt which was on the kitchen floor, Cornelius realized it belonged to one of the security personnel as the logo of the security company was on it. Without letting the security know his next move, Cornelius secretly called the boss of the security to come immediately to the scene of crime. Fifteen minutes later, the senior patrol officer with other two senior officials arrived. When the guards on duty saw their bosses at that time of the night, they were puzzled. Their fear worsened when they saw the bosses talking to Cornelius. The order which followed was to shut the door and to do a post-check. During that check, it was noticed that one of the security guards called Mamali was nowhere to be found. When the attendance register was checked, he was scheduled for night duty. This disappearance brought great concern as the senior patrol officers wanted to know where the missing guard was. When they pressurized the other guards, one of them went to the nearby house to fetch him. Full of burnt engine oil and charcoal which was what they usually applied on their skins whenever they had nocturnal activities, Mamali was brought to the authorities. Cornelius was very shocked to know that it was a guard whom he had put much confidence. Cornelius would never fail to give him tips every morning before he left his house. On one occasion, Cornelius had given Mamali some money to take care of his ailing mother who was at the point of death in the hospital as he thought that saving the life of Mamali's mother would be good seeing that he had the means of helping him. When Mamali saw Cornelius standing by, he hid his face and started crying. He felt sad that his boss who had reposed so much confidence in him had found out that he was not trustworthy. This led him to start pleading for mercy. When interrogated further, he confessed that some boys in a *clic group* had told him and two other men in the area that Cornelius was a very rich man and due to that, they should steal some of his wealth in order for them to become rich overnight.

Cornelius could not believe his ears while Mamali was revealing how it all happened. He ordered Mamali's immediate dismissal and for his own safety that night, he requested the senior patrol officers not to go away until the damaged door was fixed the following morning before his departure to America.

Very early the following morning, Cornelius called Alison to explain the unfortunate incident which occurred during the night. She was taken aback and the first question she asked was:

"Are you alright? If not, try and see the doctor immediately before you travel. After all, your flight is scheduled for the afternoon"

Cornelius thanked her for the concern but assured that he was quite ok as he was not hurt. When the news was announced to his parents, Modupeh was perturbed and she asked many questions. She further suggested that he should not leave the apartment empty in his absence as they could not know what else would happen. For that reason, she told her son to drop his keys at their house on his way to the airport and she would find someone reliable to stay in his apartment until he returned. Being an obedient son, Cornelius did not object and did as his mother had suggested. When he left his parents' house for the airport, Modupeh thought about a devoted member of their church. Henry had been extremely faithful and obedient in the church and even though he was not from a very rich family he was content and godly. She wasted no time in calling him and he was very happy to hear that. Late in the afternoon, Henry went to see Mrs. Modupeh Cole who handed the keys to him.

The flight to America was long and tedious and, as a result of not being able to sleep the previous night, Cornelius took advantage of sleeping on board the flight. He only ate once and slept until it was announced that the flight was touching down in Amsterdam which was the transit point. After three hours of transit in Amsterdam, passengers boarded another plane for Dulles airport in America. From that point, Cornelius had to take another plane to California which was another four hours of flying. When he eventually arrived in California,

Cornelius was feeling more and more tired. In fact the jet lag had a negative impact on him and he slept all the way to his hotel.

The conference started the following day and guests were in very high spirit. Cornelius' presentation was to take place during the Wednesday session. Meanwhile, Cornelius tried his best in networking with other participants at the conference. After his presentation, many of the participants commended Cornelius for a brilliant presentation. A Chief Executive Officer from a film company in Miami approached him and asked whether he would be willing to work for them. Being in a state of shock at what the CEO had said, Cornelius just told him that he would give an answer by the end of the conference which was three days away.

When he returned to his bedroom, Cornelius engaged in a half night of prayer seeking God's approval concerning the offer. The following day, he decided to fast until lunch and after the day's session he again retired to his room to pray. That night, he had a revelation from God while sleeping and it was clear that he should accept the offer. Before giving his consent to the Chief Executive Officer, Cornelius called his parents to announce the good news. His father, who always wanted the best for him, supported him and when his mother was given the phone she asked so many questions about the job offer before she finally consented. Alison son was not too pleased as the job offer did not cover spouses or any other relative but after some minutes of persuasion, she finally consented that Cornelius accept the offer. He finally informed the Chief Executive Officer that he would accept the job and when the job description was shown Cornelius could not believe his eyes; the salary was thrice what he was earning and other benefits including monthly travelling to see relatives back home were in the package. He only made an humble request to be given a month before starting the new job as he would like to hand over duty in a seamless manner. With that, he shook hands with the CEO and promised to keep in close touch.